The Furricious Gang

SURREY

Of Godalming

Book 3

A children's book for grown ups

Martyn MacDonald Adams

1St Edition 2022
MMA Associates

ISBN-13: 978-1-7396924-7-6

Illustrations by Lisa Sacchi

Editor Alan Barker

DEDICATION

For Murray of London Songwriters, for arranging his song writing retreats, and to Arvon for their writers' retreats. These are times when one can meet the most interesting, and fun, people and even learn something too.

CONTENTS

Humphrey, Jeffrey and Godfrey

The Rescue

"Bum! Bum! Daaah dih. Bum! Bum! Doooh dah…"

"Jeffrey!"

"Bum! Bum! Daaah dih. Bum! Bum! Doooh dah…"

"*Jeffrey!*"

"Tickle meeeh… Tickle yoooh… Cuddle herrrr… Huge bum!"

Slap!

"Ow!"

"Shush!"

"But it *is* a bit like *Mission Impossible*, isn't it?"

"Yes. But there's no need to sing the theme music. We've got to be quiet. We've got to be as quiet as quiet ninja mice wearing little woolly socks, squeak-free gloves, and soundproof knickers, while trying to be as quiet as they can."

"Uh. Okay. So, no squeaking."

It was a cold, dark night and Humphrey, a feral teddy bear living in Godalming, was dressed in his newly tailored

Patent Black Ninja Special Forces Stealth Mission Apparel (Size: Very Small). He lay prone underneath a hedge and alongside him was his young, slightly shorter padawan, Jeffrey, also a teddy bear. The two were dressed in a similar fashion – in fact, Jeffrey was dressed in the offcuts from the original uniform. This is possible, because these teddy bears are quite small. In fact, there was still enough material remaining for the third, even smaller, teddy bear.

They were here, in the dead of night, to rescue that third bear – the third member of the Furricious Gang, called Godfrey.

"Is it time to move out yet?" asked Jeffrey.

Humphrey glanced at his Patent Black Ninja Special Forces Stealth Wrist Chronometer and pressed the button. The screen lit up the underside of the bush in a vivid red laser light, and blinded both bears at the same time as the time, 03:38, was etched onto their retinas. It appeared to them in a vivid green afterimage amongst the dots for several minutes. In fact, for a short moment, the back of the house behind them displayed BE:EO for all the street to see.

A few minutes later, once his eyes had stopped smarting and he had dabbed away the tears (with one of his Patent Black Ninja Special Forces Absorbent Ocular Tissues), the senior bear reached into his Patent Black Ninja Special Forces Equipment Transporting Pouch and pulled out the Patent Black Ninja Special Forces Low Light Scoping Device - Mark 3.

He switched it on and looked across the dark garden and spotted two dogs, side by side, in their kennels.

Unbeknownst to Humphrey, the two dogs had spotted the
two bears a good while earlier. But then, so had all the rest

of the local wildlife.

"What was that light? Shouldn't we raise the alarm?" whispered the first dog, a cross between a Chihuahua and an apparently quite slow Dachshund.

The other dog, a cross between the same frisky Chihuahua and a very surprised Labrador, laughed.

"I dunno. Just ignore them. It's the Furricious Gang up to something daft again. They are completely harmless and besides, if we raise the alarm, we'll just get a bucket of water thrown over us. Just keep quiet and pretend like we didn't see them."

Humphrey turned to Jeffrey and whispered, "They haven't seen us yet. We'll have to go around them."

Jeffrey nodded his agreement, unsure what Humphrey meant.

Reaching into his Patent Black Ninja Special Forces Stealth Equipment Transporting Pouch, Humphrey extracted a pistol-gripped thing that looked like a small hand-held crossbow. He extracted a large coil of rope with a grappling hook at one end and fitted it into the top of the device.

Jeffrey watched him and quietly sang to himself...

"Tickle meeeh... Tickle yoooh... Cuddle herrrr... Huge..."

"Shush! Here! Grab the end. I'm going to shoot this at that shed over there."

Humphrey pointed into the middle distance, then held the pistol grip in both paws and took careful aim. His aim was so careful that his tongue came out to help by stroking his nose. He pulled the trigger.

BLUNCK!

The recoil threw Humphrey backwards. He did a one-and-a-half somersault, landing on his head with an, "Ow! I bit my thung!"

Jeffrey vanished in blur.

It took a moment for Humphrey to collect his senses.

"Jeffrey?" He looked around him. Jeffrey wasn't to be seen. "Jeffrey?" he called again, but there was no answer.

Humphrey picked up his Patent Black Ninja Special Forces Low Light Scoping Device - Mark 3 and looked through it. He had completely missed the shed and instead the grapple had landed on the roof of a house. Dangling beneath it was the rope, still coiled up, and holding on to that for grim life, was a wide-eyed Jeffrey.

"Rats!" exclaimed Humphrey.

"Rubbish!" came an unexpected reply.

Humphrey froze.

"They had nuffink to do with it. You can't shoot for toffee, you can't."

Humphrey looked down at a pair of hedgehogs.

"You're as h-accurate as a randy one-eyed h-otter falling over a waterfall with his eye closed h-after h-ogling a lady h-otter and then being bashed on the 'ead by her boyfriend."

"Uhm... Uhm... that's very... specific."

"Yeh. Made us laugh, didn't it, Knuckles?"

The other hedgehog laughed. "Yeh. That kept me laughing for the rest of the week, Spudgun. Made my day that did."

The two hedgehogs ambled off leaving Humphrey temporarily confused.

Humphrey pressed the little button on his Patent Black Ninja Special Forces Stealth Radio Communications Earbud.

"Jeffrey? Jeffrey? Do you copy?"

"No! I can't copy anything. I'm stuck on a roof! Help!"

"Okay, okay. I can see you. Don't panic. I'm coming over to you now."

Humphrey gathered up his kit and stuffed it all into the pouch, and scurried across the garden, through another hedge, across a small car park and up to the house.

The two dogs watched the bear with interest.

"What's he up to now?" asked the Chihuahua-Dachshund.

"Dunno. He just launched his little friend onto the top of Mr. B's house. Bears are weird."

Humphrey pressed the little button on his earbud again.

"Jeffrey. Jeffrey. I am underneath you. Unravel the rope and climb down it. I'll meet you on the ground."

Jeffrey, still gripping the end of the rope, reached up and unclipped the clips that kept the coiled coils coiled. They sprang free and Jeffrey slid down the roof, bounced off the gutter, and ever so gracefully cartwheeled earthward. He hit something soft and bounced onto the lawn, still gripping the end of the rope.

"Ooof!" said the now semi-conscious Humphrey, dazed by Jeffrey's impact. He fell over onto his back.

Jeffrey stood up, relieved to be on firm ground once again. He noticed a button he had not seen earlier, several centimetres from the end of the rope. Not knowing what it did, he pressed it, but nothing seemed to happen.

Up on the roof, the hooks on the grappling hook retracted and it fell away, making a scratching sound as it slid down the roof tiles, before striking the gutter with a loud clunk and then falling to earth to land on something soft, and gently bouncing away onto the lawn.

"Gurple!" said the now brained bear.

Jeffrey walked up to Humphrey who was clutching his head, his eyes were spinning.

"Humpy, what does this button do?" He held up the rope.

Once his vision cleared and he'd been able to catch his breath, the bruised bear's response was not only unrepeatable, but it was not ninja stealthy in the slightest.

Jeffrey, however, did learn a lot of new, mostly four-letter, words and their derivatives.

As soon as Humphrey had almost recovered, the two teddy bears dashed across the King's Road, past the parked cars, and on to the houses on the far side. But Humphrey, still dazed from being the target of various plummeting objects, found himself continually veering to the right and so had to stop and reorient himself to compensate.

The street was dark with only a couple of street lamps lit. The bears kept to the shadows, or in Humphrey's case, tried to keep to the shadows.

There was only one window with a light showing, and that belonged to a nosey old lady who knew all about the teddy bears of Godalming. She'd lived in the town for decades and had caught sight of them many years ago, but trying to explain this to her neighbours had proved futile. They thought she was senile but, being ever so polite, never said so to her face. They just agreed with her. So, when she saw the two bears run past her house, she thought everyone knew of their existence. She didn't feel the need to take a photo of them but wondered if they would appreciate a saucer of milk and maybe some biscuits.

They would have. Especially the biscuits.

A fox stepped out from the shadows.

"What are you two up to, all dressed up in black?"

"Oh. Hello, Barnaby. You frightened me," said Humphrey. "We're here to rescue Godfrey. He's been kidnapped by a child."

The fox nodded. "Is your cat friend, Snowy, around?"

"No. She's off looking for bats. According to the owls, they've been deliberately flying onto people's heads and stealing wigs and hair extensions. It's causing a bit of an uproar amongst the humans. The Avian Musicians Union has categorised it as a Hair Traffic Control problem."

"Good," said Barnaby. "We don't exactly get along."

Humphrey nodded. That was true.

"I'll see you about. Humphrey. Jeffrey."

"Bye," said Humphrey.

"Bye," waved Jeffrey.

With that, the fox trotted off, watched warily by both bears. Barnaby had a bit of a reputation.

"Tickle meeeh... Tickle yoooh... Cuddle herrrr... Huge..."

"Stop it!"

"Sorry."

The bears slipped between the bins, and up to a wooden gate. Humphrey stood with his back to it and cupped his paws.

"This is the one. Leg up!"

Jeffrey deftly jumped up, then stood on Humphrey's head to reach up to the top of the fence, before tumbling over the other side and landing on the ground with a grunt.

"Twit! Now how am I going to get over this gate? You were supposed to stay on top and help pull me up."

Jeffrey opened the gate a crack and peered around it at Humphrey, who looked up at the top and scratched his head.

"Sorry," said Jeffrey. "Let's try it again."

"No," said Humphrey. "This time you cup your hands, and I'll leap onto the gate. I'll show you how it should be done."

"Okay." Jeffrey stood with his back to the wood just as Humphrey had earlier, and Humphrey leapt up, stepping on Jeffrey's head to lie across the top of the gate, precariously balanced but narrowly avoiding toppling off.

"Here," he said. "That's the way to do it."

"Okay," said Jeffrey, who then pushed the gate open and went through. The bottom of the gate caught on a stone and Humphrey tumbled off to land beside the younger bear. He stood up and dusted himself down.

"So, it's open already?" he sighed.

"Tickle meeeh..." sang Jeffrey, as he ran up the garden path to the back door, oblivious to Humphrey's embarrassment.

Humphrey arrived a few seconds later.

"How do we get in?" whispered Jeffrey.

"Skeleton keys," whispered Humphrey, as he rattled a bunch of bent metal rods.

Jeffrey stood with his back against the back door, while Humphrey again clambered up onto his head. Humphrey poked and twisted each of the bent rods in the keyhole until the lock opened, then he grabbed the door handle and the door swung open, outwards, knocking Jeffrey over. Humphrey fell to the ground too.

From the kitchen came a deep growl.

"Uh oh!" said Humphrey, starting to tremble. "Uhm sorry? We didn't mean to disturb anyone."

The growling continued.

"Uhm-m-m. P-please don't bark. We're not here to r-rob you."

The growling got louder. Humphrey took a step back.

"We-we're h-here to r-rescue Godfrey. He's a teddy bear. A c-cute little chap. A bit c-clumsy. He f-fell off a tree and a little child picked him up and took him home b-by accident."

The growling continued.

"H-he's not a *toy* teddy bear. He's a real one. He's one of us. P-please can we have him back?"

The growling stopped. Thinking that some sort of progress had been made, Humphrey tried the diplomatic approach.

"M-my name is Humpy-Humphrey, and this here is…" Humphrey turned to look for Jeffrey, but he was nowhere to be seen. "Jeffrey. Jeffrey? W-where are you?"

The garden gate, which had been open, but was now closed, opened a little. Jeffrey peered around it and waved.

"Hullo," came the little voice from the end of the garden. He waved a paw.

Remembering the contents of his rescue kit, Humphrey unzipped his Patent Black Ninja Special Forces Stealth Thigh-Pouch (Water resistant. Size: Very Small) and pulled out a tin opener and dropped it.

"You do like meat, don't you? Silly me. All g-guard dogs like meat."

He picked up the tin opener, pulled out a tin of dog food and started opening it. As soon as the lid was open, he lobbed it through the back door and into the dark shadows of the kitchen. It landed with a clunk. It was then that he remembered he should have emptied the can onto the floor before covering it with the sleeping drug he had in one of his Patent Black Ninja Special Forces Stealth Belt-Pouches (Water resistant. Size: Very Small).

"Oops," he said. "Uhm, c-can I have the c-can back? I didn't d-do that properly." It was then that he realised he might have hit the dog with it, which couldn't possibly have made things any better.

But the tin did not come back. And the growling did not start again. Had he knocked the dog unconscious? If so, he needed to move fast.

Cautiously, Humphrey approached the back step and took out his Patent Black Ninja Special Forces Stealth Pepper Spray (Food Flavouring – also available in flavours: mustard, brown sauce, mint sauce, and ketchup). Then he extracted his Patent Black Ninja Special Forces Hand-Held Environment Illuminating Device from its holster, and switched it on. The torch lit up the kitchen floor with over two thousand lumens, enough to temporarily blind any guard dog, completely dazzle the bear, and let everyone in King's Road know that there was currently a break-in in progress.

So much for Ninja Special Forces subtlety.

After a moment, his eyes adapted to the bright light and he could see the open tin on its side at the far end of the kitchen floor untouched, and also no guard dog. He switched the light off, but now he had the opposite problem. Everything went pitch-black as his eyes attempted a quick U-turn to adapt to the dark again.

"Grrrrrr..."

So, the beast was still awake and ready to pounce. Humphrey extended his paw with the pepper spray and

14

slowly edged into the kitchen, ready to squirt it into the glaring red eyes of the guard dog of death.

"Grrrrrr..."

Humphrey stopped. The sound came from above him. He looked up. 'My God!' he thought. This monster was nearly two metres tall! No wonder it wasn't interested in such a small tin of dog food!

"Grrrrrr..."

At this point, Humphrey's bravery was trumped by a desperate need to pee. He turned and ran out of the kitchen, veered to his right (he was still suffering from the earlier head trauma), found a bush to hide behind, and started to relieve himself.

"What are you doing?" asked Godfrey.

Humphrey almost had a seizure, spun around, and watered the garden.

"Yeuch! You wetted me!"

"S-sorry, Jeffrey... Godfrey? I thought you were the guard dog."

"No. I'm not a dog. I'm Godfrey. I'm a bear! Now I'm a wetted bear. Bwah! You weed on me! Yeuch!"

"Guard dogs don't like being weed upon either!" advised Jeffrey. "You should use the mustard spray instead."

"Jeffrey? I thought you were at the gate?"

Through the dim light, Humphrey could just make out the profiles of the two teddy bears. He hastily tidied himself up.

"No. I was, then I saw Godfrey at the bedroom window, so I climbed up the drainpipe and opened it. Godfrey and I escaped."

"Where's the guard dog?" asked Humphrey.

"It's a parrot," said Godfrey. "His name is Black Cerberus, and he takes his job very seriously."

Humphrey nodded.

"Okay. So, mission accomplished. Let's go!"

The bears ran down the garden. Jeffrey started singing the theme music again. When he got to: "Tickle meeeh... Tickle yoooh... Cuddle herrrr... Huge bum!" Godfrey fell on the grass giggling.

The two bears stopped and watched the small one writhing about on the ground with tears in his eyes, holding his sides.

"I bet Tom Cruise never has this problem," sighed Humphrey.

Humphrey, Jeffrey and Godfrey

The Museum Trip

The three bears that live in Godalming are known as the Furricious Gang. Note that the word is Furricious and that it is not the same as Ferocious or Furious which are completely different words. The word Furricious means something a lot more giggly, cuddly, and furry.

Humphrey, the most senior of the bears, opened the door to Jeffrey's bedroom. The other two bears were busy playing with little figures on the floor.

"Okay, chaps, listen up! I have an announcement to make."

Jeffrey was at that age when he thought himself the wisest, cleverest, and most brave of the bears. He was wrong on all three counts.

"Can I listen down? We're playing," he said.

"I just want you to listen. I would like to make an announcement."

Jeffrey looked up at Humphrey.

"So why do we have to listen upwards?" Jeffrey turned his attention back to the game. It looked like it was going to be one of those nit-picking arguments bears of a certain age like to indulge in. Humphrey sighed and decided to continue anyway.

"How would you two chaps like to go on a picnic?"

"It's too cold," said Jeffrey.

"Not if the picnic is indoors."

"You mean lunch?"

"No. I mean a real picnic."

"I'm busy," said Jeffrey.

"What are you playing?"

Godfrey was the youngest of the three bears. He thought that he was not the wisest, not the cleverest, and not the bravest of the three. He was wrong on at least one count.

"We're playing pink-a-nick logi... can... of... lipsticks," said Godfrey.

Jeffrey laughed, but didn't say anything.

Humphrey thought for a moment. "You mean, picnic logistics?"

"That's what I said."

"Yes. That's a very important game. How to select, acquire, and then transport the most food the furthest, to the best spot, and with the least possible effort." Humphrey was impressed. "A very educational game for teddy bears."

"We need a monk jack," stated Godfrey.

"Pardon?"

"He means, we need a muntjac," said Jeffrey. "Or two."

"Do you mean those cute little deer that can sometimes be seen in the Lammas Lands?"

"Yes."

"Why?"

"Because they can carry our food in backpacks, and they only eat grass."

Godfrey held up a little figure of a muntjac. "And they don't like chocolate biscnits, and they don't bash you with their horns, and they don't go 'moo' or 'baa'," he said. "Do they like gravy on their grass?"

Jeffrey laughed again. "No. They like their salad undressed."

"Do they take their coats off to eat then?"

Jeffrey laughed again, but said nothing.

Humphrey pondered the idea. "That's a good thought. I'll have to remember that next time we go on a picnic there. Employ naked muntjacs as pack animals."

Everything went silent for a moment, so Humphrey tried again.

"I'm thinking we could visit the museum in Convent Garden this afternoon."

Both young bears stopped what they were doing and looked up at Humphrey.

"What is a mesuem?" asked Godfrey.

"The *museum* is a part of UCL, or the Ursine Central Library. It's a place where teddy bears can learn about things that teddy bears need to learn about. Our culture, science, and our history."

"What sort of things?"

"Well, there are stories about pirates, like Edward Black Eared, the notorious pirate of the Bristol Channel (summer season only). There are stories about the teddy bear space programme, and the first bear to picnic on top of Everest who also happens to be the fastest bear to come down a mountain - albeit inside a huge snowball; he also holds the record for being the dizziest bear for the longest time, even after they eventually thawed him out.

"Then there's information about how submarines work, who invented the light bulb, who invented the heavy bulb, how we managed to control cold fusion, but only after sinking a place called Atlantis – which is our biggest "oops" moment in history. How we discovered that an iceberg can easily sink unsinkable steam ships, like the Titanic. Although some naughty polar bears were also responsible for that one.

"Then there was the discovery of unpowered flight by the Bright Brothers, and how the Bright Sisters learnt how to treat lots of broken bones. Electricity was invented by young Freddy Bear, later to become the first teddy bear rap artist - Frazzled Freddy, The Freaky Furry Frizzball."

Jeffrey was warming to the idea. "It's a good place. The restaurant has lots of stuff."

Humphrey continued, "They even hold political debates there, like: should we be right-wing and conquer the human race? Force them to be our slaves and make snacks for us? Or instead, can we teach them the importance of a good, civilised picnic? Should our Mars colonies greet Elon Musk with a table of snacks? If we do, should we insist that he brings his own biscuits to share? And if so, should he start his own electric space-chocolate biscuit company first? Lots and lots of exciting stuff like that."

Godfrey was uncertain. "Has it got unicorns, dinosnores, and allingators?"

Jeffrey guffawed. "Dinosnores!"

"Yes. In the natural history sections, although I'm not too sure about the unicorns. They're still pretty upset after we sank Atlantis. But we get to go to Convent Garden by underground train."

Godfrey's eyes lit up. "I've not been on a nun-derground train before."

"Well, actually, you have. We went to Borough Hall once when you were a very tiny baby bear. Jeffrey had you in his backpack which he converted into a baby carrier, but he put you in it upside down, so you didn't see very much. It did make everyone laugh a lot though. Your little legs waggling up in the air."

"Not everyone," sulked Jeffrey.

"Ah yes. I forgot. While you were upside down, you managed to find Jeffrey's biscuit tin and scoffed all of his travel snacks. That was how you stayed quiet the whole trip. Jeffrey wanted me to sell you when he found out."

Now, at this point I need to explain something. Running through, or rather under, the town of Godalming is a part of the animals' underground railway network, known as The Electric Subway for Little Animals, or TESLA for short – not to be confused with other organisations. It was constructed by the moles on behalf of the hedgehogs, who have great fun managing it. They love to buy and sell tickets and drive the trains. Rabbits and mice help out a lot too. The mice are particularly skilful at making and maintaining the trains and the barriers.

The lines actually reach all across the country. Godalming lies at a junction between the Reading to Brighton Line and the London to Portsmouth Line. So, the local stations on the Brighton Line (north to south) are Chalk Road, Embankment, Borough Hall Junction, Bank, Holloway Hill, Park Road, and Convent Garden (near Ladywell Convent).

On the London to Portsmouth Line (west to east) the local stations are Godalming, St. Pauls, Borough Hall Junction, Supermarket, and Woodside Park.

It is rumoured that humans, often stuck as to what to name their own railway stations, copied some of their ideas from the hedgehogs. Of course, they absolutely deny this.

While Humphrey had been talking, Jeffrey had got up and disappeared into his own bedroom and then returned dressed, packed, and ready to go. As soon as Godfrey realised this, he started to scramble about, getting ready to go too.

As Humphrey turned to leave the room, he suggested that Jeffrey advise Godfrey on what was suitable to take. For instance, the Scalextric set, the snorkel, and his football boots were probably not good ideas.

Before they set off, the gang had a light pre-pre-picnic-snack lunch. Humphrey also used that time to pack a pre-picnic-snack pack, then off they went.

From where they lived, close to the Jack Phillips Memorial, the journey to Godalming Station wasn't very far. They waited until the coast was clear and then dashed across Borough Road, up Vicarage Walk, across Westbrook Road, and into the bushes where the animals had their secret entrance to Godalming Station. This is very close to where the humans have their own Godalming Station, which, in the view of the animals, should really have been called Godalming Station Station, as the animals had got there first. But humans are such an unreasonable species; just ask the dodos, woolly mammoths, or the tasty Timid Turtles of Tiverton.

"Where would you like to go?" asked the hedgehog, at the ticket office.

"Hello, Thaddeus. Three bears to Convent Garden, please." Humphrey held up his travel pass.

"Oooh. A day out at the museum, is it? How exciting." He looked at a table on the wall and then cross-checked with a printed book. Then he checked with a leaflet before consulting another book. "Well, today is a 'Blue Tuesday' in

March and you're a local family of bears with a green second-class travel pass... travelling off-peak... with no bicycles... and no silly hats... does anyone have a gammy leg?"

"No," replied Humphrey.

"Okay. So, there's a thirty percent discount. That'll be twelve biscuits for all three of you, but you get free admission to the museums and a complimentary snack if you come back and do this again on a 'Yellow Thursday' before autumn, when travelling off-peak with an extra bear, unless there's an 'r' in the month or you're wearing a silly hat."

"How do you remember all these rules?"

The hedgehog shrugged and grinned. "It's fun."

"It's sad," said Humphrey, not meaning to have said that out loud. Thaddeus stopped smiling and stamped the tickets very hard.

Humphrey paid up and the bears followed the signs to Platform One. When they arrived, there was already a family of rabbits and a group of mice in silly hats further up the platform.

On the ceiling was a sign, which read, 'The next train arrives in two minutes and stops at all stations to London Waterloo North, so it takes a long while to get there. This is a new yellow one with only two stiff windows, one bumpy wheel, and a dirty seat, otherwise it is quite clean. The driver's name is Henrietta. She is married, likes to go swimming, and she whistles when she drives, which can be quite annoying if you are sitting right at the front.'

One of the baby bunnies bounded up to Godfrey.

"Hello," she said. "My name is Tinkleberry."

"Hullo," said Godfrey. "We're going to the mesuem."

"Oh. We're going to Clapham."

"Clap who?"

"Clap-ham."

"Pigs *are* very clever," mused Godfrey, unsure as to why else the rabbits would applaud them. For instance, there are not many porcine pop idols. Their ability to sing, if you can call it that, is not one of their most appealing attributes. They even struggle with rap, which is quite an achievement.

"Yes, they are," said the bunny, unsure as to why the bear had suddenly changed the subject to pigs.

Tinkleberry, now feeling a little less sure of herself, decided it was far safer to remain close to Mummy and so hopped back. Her mother bent down after Tinkleberry poked her in the ribs, and whispered into one of Mum's large ears. Godfrey heard her mum say, "That is what they call a non-sequitur, darling."

Godfrey got a little upset. He was a bear, surely a rabbit mum knew that! Silly rabbits. And for several months after that, Tinkleberry thought that non-sequiturs looked remarkably like teddy bears.

The train pulled into the station with a loud moan that got lower and lower and quieter and quieter as the train slowed to a stop. Then, it seemed to slowly sneeze its doors open with a sort of foo-slish-shoo-bump type of sound.

The bears boarded the carriage and found some empty seats. The train slowly sneezed its doors shut with another foo-slish-shoo-bump, and accelerated into the dark tunnel.

"Humpy, do scribbles like the mesuem?" asked Godfrey.

"No. The only culture scribbles have is bacteria-based."

"Oh," he said, and then sat mesmerised at the window watching the power cables attached to the sides of the tunnel as they seemed to dance up and down.

"What are we going to see?" asked Jeffrey.

"I thought we'd visit some of the oxymoronic departments."

"What do you mean?"

"Well, there's Lost Discoveries, Advanced Primitive Species, Famous Restored Ruins, New Ancient Artifacts, The Civil War, Modern History, and other stuff like that."

"Is there any stuff to do with space?"

"Oh yes. You'll find 'authentic models' of spacecraft on 'permanent loan' in the 'Individual Collections' department." Humphrey frowned. "They really do love their oxymorons, don't they? I wonder if it's a game the curators like to play."

The bears changed train at Borough Hall, and proceeded south to Convent Garden. There was an entrance to the museum near the platform, and the trio went down another tunnel and then passed into the museum foyer. Standing as the centre piece in the foyer was a huge skeleton of a Tyrannosaurus Rex.

"Wow!" said Jeffrey.

"Woh! That's new," said Humphrey.

"But I don't want to be eatened!" wailed Godfrey.

Jeffrey laughed. "He can't eat you. He's a skeleton."

"Do skellingtons eat bears?"

"No. He's dead."

Godfrey paused for a moment, then he said, "Awww. Why did they kill him?"

Humphrey smiled. "We didn't kill her. She's been dead for millions of years."

Godfrey looked confused.

Jeffrey grabbed Godfrey's paw. "Come on, let's look at the pictures," and he pulled the young bear to look at the sign boards. There were several artists' impressions of what they thought the dinosaur looked like when it was alive. Had the dinosaur seen what they'd drawn though, she would have been horrified. She had been very sensitive about the size of her bottom.

Several minutes later, both bears returned, grabbed Humphrey, and dragged him to the Natural History section,

which was full of life-sized models of animals and,
thankfully, nothing to do with history.

Then Godfrey spotted an open door at the side of the gallery.

"What's in there?"

"Don't know," said Jeffrey.

So, Godfrey went in to explore. Inside was a steep staircase leading down.

Many minutes later a museum security badger came across two very wet bears standing forlornly in one of the access corridors. Both looked really miserable and were dripping water onto the floor.

"Hello there. What do we have here? Two lost bears that seem to have fallen into our flooded basement. It's full of water in there, you know. We've had a burst water pipe."

"We know," said Jeffrey. "We found out."

"We slipped on the top step and fell in. We're all wetted now," said Godfrey.

"Here, come with me and I'll dry you off."

"We mustn't go with strange animals. It might make Humphrey unhappy."

"Well, you can't stand there waiting for Humphrey all wet and miserable, can you? You might catch a cold. Let me take you to the infirmary and I can dry you off."

Jeffrey thought a moment. "Alright, but it might make Humphrey unhappy."

The infirmary was only a couple of corridors away, and the badger and a nurse hedgehog gave the two bears a good rub down with nice clean towels and dried them off.

Godfrey's tummy rumbled.

"I see we have two hungry teddy bears, don't we?" declared the security badger. "How about I take you both to the canteen for a nice hot drink and even a snack or two?"

Jeffrey thought a moment. "Alright, but it might make Humphrey very unhappy."

The badger led them to the canteen where the two bears got a mug of nice hot chocolate each. Each mug had cream sprayed on top and chocolate powder and sprinkles sprinkled on top of that, which they absolutely loved. Then they had some chocolate bourbon biscuits and some chocolate digestives as well, and then they finished the mini feast with a jam tart each.

"There. You must feel a lot better now, don't you?"

"Yes. Thank you," nodded Jeffrey.

"Oh yes. Thank you very, very, very much. It was very nice." Godfrey wiped some chocolate from his nose with a tissue. "Especially the sprinkly bits."

"Now then," said the security badger, "I must return you to your guardian. Who would that be?"

"His name is Humphrey. But I think he will be very unhappy." Jeffrey folded up his napkin neatly.

"Just tell your Humphrey that we looked after you and that we treated you very well. I'm sure he'll understand."

"Okay. I still think he will be very unhappy though."

"Oh? And why is that?"

"He's still waiting for us to pull him out of the basement," said Godfrey.

Humphrey, Jeffrey and Godfrey

The Biscuit Machine

Humphrey, Jeffrey and Godfrey, the three teddy bears known as Godalming's Furricious Gang, were returning from an early morning walk along the river Wey. Humphrey suddenly stopped and looked at the field above their underground home.

"Oh no. Moles!"

Two moles were patting down a molehill. Humphrey walked across to them.

"Hello," he said.

"You must be our new neighbour. We're moving in here."

"So I see, but I have to tell you that the council frowns upon moles in this park. It's dedicated to a chap called Jack Phillips. You will be..."

The mole laughed. "No, no, no, no, no. You've got it all wrong, mate. The council won't care. If we keep our hills quite small and don't spoil the grass too much, they'll leave us alone." He grinned. "My name is Fairbanks, this 'ere is Douglas."

"I'm sure the council will come along and..."

"Nope. They won't. We're here to stay."

"How do you know?"

"Because we have a spy, a 'mole' you might say, in the council offices we have." The two moles laughed at their little joke. "A mole, see. We're moles and we have a mole in their offices." The two moles found that very funny and laughed even more, slapping each other on the back. "Funny, innit!"

Then the smaller one spoke up.

"They haven't got much budget for parks. And we know everything they're saying because we have bugs in their offices too. So, provided we don't make too much of a mess we are quite safe... neighbour."

"You've got insects in their offices too?"

"No, you idiot. Bugs. Little electronic devices for listening."

"Oh." Humphrey was a little perplexed.

"Do you like music?"

"Yes...?"

"Then you'll like our heavy metal rock band, because we like to PAAARTY!!!" The two moles did a little dance, laughed and slapped each other on the back again. "And you won't mind us if our tunnels connect, will you? We're very sociable moles. We like to share. You don't mind if we borrow your kitchen, do you? We're holding a housewarming party this weekend and you're more than welcome."

"Yeh. But bring your own earplugs because we like to party LOUD!!! See yah!" said the little mole.

The two moles dived into the hole and then disguised the hill from the inside so you could hardly tell it was there.

"Oh no," said Humphrey quietly, turning pale and looking more and more like a polar bear.

***

That night Benjamin, a.k.a. The Brutal Badger of Binscombe, stood in the shadows behind the block of flats in front of a metal garage door. He looked at the scribble standing in front of him. His small dark eyes narrowed making him look as evil as his reputation. It was night-time, and the moisture from both animals' breath briefly condensed into vapour before drifting away into the cold night air. Benjamin's lips curled inward, just a little, but enough to show his fangs. It was unclear if it was the cold or fear that made the smaller animal shake.

"You did what?"

The scribble, a scrawny squirrel-like animal, squirmed. Her nearly bald tail twitched in fear.

"We stole... stole an entire carton of biscuits from the supermarket. So, if you want some, we can supply them to you for half price... if you want."

"Scribbles are stupid. You know that?"

"But we've got the biscuits. I thought you said you needed them for a party."

"I need them for a meeting with the otters. The Surrey Badgers are thinking of twinning with Lyme Regis and they're getting together to discuss the visit from the West Dorset Otters. We need biscuits and fish to grease the wheels. Do you understand? Did you get any fish?"

"No fish. Sorry. We only eat nuts. Squirrels' nuts usually... but not yours. We wouldn't eat your nuts... we wouldn't even touch your nuts... not even lick... unless you wanted us to... I bet you have nice nuts... uhm..." There was an awkward pause. "That didn't come out right. Look, we've only got the biscuits we stole. Besides, Emperor Plasticene tried to get you some frozen salmon fillets, but he fell into the freezer and now he's a popsicle."

"You know the Furricious Gang are manufacturing their own biscuits now, don't you?"

"Uhm... No?"

"They've offered me several packets at a *tenth* the price."

The scribble's tail twitched in anger.

"But those bears make distilled beetfruit, not biscuits."

"They're branching out. They are very industrious little bears, they are. If you can match their price, I'll consider it. Until then, well, I'll see you about... won't I." And with that Benjamin trotted off into the darkness.

The scribble squeaked in fear, frustration, and anger, which are a lot of emotions for a little scribble to handle.

***

Early next morning Humphrey, the leader of the Furricious Gang, was clearing away the breakfast table when he heard a knock at the door.

"I wonder who that could be," he called out, quite loudly, and shuffled toward the front door while untying his pink floral pinafore. He peered through the peephole. "My goodness, it is the scribbles; I wonder what they could want." There was a scuffle from inside the underground home as the other two bears dashed from their bedrooms and ran down the hall.

"Who is it?" called out Humphrey through the door.

"It's us!"

"Hello us. What do you want?"

"We want to see if you have a biscuit machine."

"We do. Yes."

"Can we see it?"

"No. It's a secret. No-one knows we have one."

There was a short pause while the scribbles squabbled amongst themselves.

Then, "We wish to buy some biscuits from you."

"Oh good," said Humphrey, "because we have lots to sell. We make them, you know."

"Can you open the door?"

Humphrey tossed the pinafore to one side and opened the front door.

"Please come in, gentlemen. Let us talk business."

Five scribbles walked in, two stood guard outside. The leader of the scribbles was a little indignant. "I am not a gentleman. I am a lady! These other four are men-scribbles," she declared.

"No gentlemen then. I'm sorry, I was mistaken, but do come in anyway."

"Is it true you are making biscuits now?" The leader of the group stood upright and looked at Humphrey squarely at his right nipple - or where his right nipple would be if he had one. Being a teddy bear, he didn't of course but his height did make him feel superior to the little greasy creature.

"Yes. We have a secret biscuit-making machine."

"Do you realise you are making our stash of biscuits worthless? We recently stole... uhm, acquired, a whole carton of biscuits. It cost us a lot in bribes, and now your biscuits will make all of that pointless."

"Well, that's progress for you."

"I'd like to see it."

"We don't do tours of our secret biscuit factory. People might become jealous and want to steal our biscuit-making machine. To do that they would only need to tunnel their way down a few feet through the grass above, and then lift the machine out and then they would be very rich, and we would have to buy all our biscuits from them. And what's worse, they could sell the biscuits they made for any price they wanted to."

The lady scribble thought for a moment before thinking of a brilliant plan to make herself rich.

"How much would it cost me to see the biscuit maker?"

"Oooh, I don't know. A lot. Half a packet of chocolate digestives?"

39

"How about half a packet of plain digestives."

"Do you have that much?"

She turned and addressed two of her accomplices. "You two, Boba Fat and Hang Solow, fetch me a half packet from the stash. Now!"

Two of the scribbles dashed outside.

While they were waiting Humphrey tried to make conversation. "Interesting names they have. They remind me of something."

"Yes. We stole... uhm, acquired, some human DVDs and ever since then these idiots have been changing their names to their heroes. It's all very childish really."

"Yes, I see. And what should I call you?"

"Layer. You can call me Princess Layer."

Humphrey nodded and thought he vaguely recognised that name too.

A few awkward minutes later the two scribbles returned, carrying a half packet of digestive biscuits.

"Excellent," said Humphrey. "Leave them in the kitchen while I take the, uhm, princess? To our new secret biscuit factory."

"You other two, wait here," commanded the self-declared royal, and the couple descended the tunnels, turning left and right through many turns, passing many doors, until they arrived at a door with a cardboard sign marked 'Bicsit Factree' in crayon.

Humphrey knocked on the door and opened it to reveal a large machine making a loud shushing noise. It had pistons moving back and forth and lots and lots of flashing lights. On the top of it were two very large pressure gauges. One was marked: Slow, Medium, Fast, Faster, and Too Fast. The other was marked: Cold, Warm, Very Warm, Hot, and Ouch! On the side was a large sign that read 'Bicsit Macking Mashene' (teddy bears are not known for their ability to spell).

Working the machine were the other two members of the Furricious Gang, Jeffrey and Godfrey. They were dressed in overalls and wearing gas masks. Godfrey stood to one side pulling and pushing a lever and making a light flash red then blue.

"Why are they wearing gas masks? Is there a poisonous gas?"

"No," smiled Humphrey. "We are teddy bears making lots of tasty biscuits. They are not gas masks; they are necessary PPE. That is, Picnic Prevention Equipment. Otherwise our production rate would be much lower and our workers much fatter. It's what we call a 'Wealth and Shapely' matter."

"Oh, I see."

They watched as Jeffrey lifted a cardboard box labelled 'In Greedy Ants' from a shelf in front of a flap labelled 'From the Where Hows'. He walked over to the machine and put it onto the conveyor belt. It disappeared inside the machine and then, after a moment, a box labelled 'Biscits' came out the other side. Jeffrey put that box onto another conveyor belt, and it disappeared through a flap labelled 'To the Where Hows'. Then he slowly walked back to the first shelf

where another box labelled 'In Greedy Ants' appeared and
he repeated the process.

"It seems very easy to operate. May I see the biscuits?"

"Yes of course. Why don't we see them as they come out of the biscuit maker?"

The pair walked up to the machine and followed Jeffrey until the box labelled 'Biscits' came out, then Humphrey took it to one side and opened it. It was full of neatly stacked dark brown biscuits.

"Bourbons. Interesting choice. May I?" the lady scribble took one and tasted it.

"Yes. Good, aren't they?"

She replaced the half-eaten biscuit and Humphrey handed the box back to Jeffrey.

"How much would you sell this biscuit maker for?"

"Oh, you know us teddy bears. We love biscuits. I'm afraid it's not for sale."

"I thought you bears liked marmalade sandwiches... Or honey."

"Oh yes. We love them too. And jam. But we're not from Peru or from the countryside. Biscuits suit us just fine."

The princess looked up at the ceiling. "Are you not frightened that someone would tunnel through the ceiling and steal this machine during the night?"

"There are already some dodgy characters up there, tunnelling away, and they are getting close, but so far they've dug everywhere except over this room. Besides, the tunnels aren't big enough. So, we're quite safe for a while. Let me show you out."

And so, Humphrey showed the scribbles out of his underground home, and he was very relieved.

***

Later that night Humphrey awoke to find his red silent alarm light flashing. He got up, put on his fluffy bunny slippers and his pink housecoat and crept round to Jeffrey's bedroom door. Jeffrey opened his bedroom door wearing his spiderman's pyjamas.

"Shush!" said Humphrey holding a paw up to his lips, then giggled.

The pair then crept down the tunnels and listened to a lot of scratching, banging, shouting, squealing, and scuffling coming from above the ceiling.

The two couldn't stop giggling.

***

Benjamin, The Brutal Badger of Binscombe, stood in the shadows behind the block of flats in front of a metal garage door. He looked at the teddy bear standing in front of him. His small dark eyes narrowed making him look as evil as his reputation. It was night-time, and the moisture from both animals' breath briefly condensed into vapour before drifting away into the cold night air. Benjamin's lips curled upward, just a little, but enough to show his smile.

"Did it work?"

Humphrey handed over two bottles of distilled beetfruit juice to the badger.

"I'd like to thank you, Benjamin. That was much appreciated."

"Two bottles?"

"Yes. The scribbles gave us some biscuits to look at our biscuit-making machine. I thought it only fair to give you a little bonus."

"Thanks. And the moles?"

"Well, the scribbles and moles fought for most of the night. In the end the moles left. They were outnumbered. The scribbles then started digging and making an absolute mess everywhere but, in the end, they gave up. They weren't sure where to dig. Besides, scribbles prefer trees or waste bins rather than squishy mud to live in. So, they've gone too. It's all peace and quiet now. I've sent a message to the scribbles saying that the biscuit machine broke down and it can't be repaired, so they won't come back.

"I've also sent a letter to the council complaining about the messy field. I'm sure that they will come and tidy it up, one day. Eventually. Maybe. I'll have to warn Godfrey that when they do, they'll probably bring a grass-muncher monster."

"A what?"

"Oh, that's another story."

"So, all turned out well then."

"Yes, but Godfrey still thinks it was a real biscuit-making machine. We keep telling him it was only pretend, but I think he's really disappointed that it can't actually make biscuits. Or current buns."

"Ha, ha. Here, have some beetfruit juice with me." Benjamin opened a bottle, and they had a swig or three each.

Benjamin hiccupped then said "I've heard that the scribbles are organising a fancy-dress party near the Old Quaker Burial Ground. I thought I'd go and give them a fright. You know, paint my white stripes red and go as Darth Mole."

Humphrey nearly fell over laughing. "Or you could go in a teddy bear outfit and call yourself Chew Badger."

The two couldn't stop giggling for quite some time.

Humphrey, Jeffrey and Godfrey

Beware the Fluffy

In the middle of a cold and moonless night, a tall pale-faced gentleman called Vladimir Laraduc moved into his new apartment in the town of Godalming. He looked out of his bedroom window and was delighted with the location. It was in a new housing estate beside a main road and conveniently close to a reputable supermarket. A supermarket where the slightly wealthier, and therefore slightly healthier, people shopped.

And better yet, that meant that the supermarket, with its convenient late opening hours, would attract the food he most desired.

People.

Plump people.

For Mr. Laraduc was a vampire.

***

The alarm clock rang out and woke Humphrey from his dream of bathing in a cosy warm bathtub of baked beans. He had been wearing his pink pinafore and blue wellington boots and smoking a rather plump courgette. His dreams were nothing if not colourful. He yawned, stretched, reached across to the alarm clock and threw it at the wall where it shattered into twenty pieces.

47

Sometimes Humphrey was a grumpy bear.

Dawn would soon be breaking and that meant he and his two fellow teddy bears would soon be out for their morning stroll by the River Wey. In practice the morning constitutional usually meant dodging behind trees and hiding behind bushes to avoid Godalming's early morning joggers. Annoyingly, there were more and more of these pests, and he wondered if the gang should move to a new home or find a way to convince people that jogging by the river was unhealthy.

He then wondered if a local gang of scribbles, known as the River Pirates of The River Wey (Godalming Branch), would be interested in terrorising the joggers, then decided against it. It would only need one dog and they'd be off.

Humphrey got up, put on his pink bathrobe and his favourite bunny slippers and, while dodging bits of broken clock, made his way to the bathroom where, as usual, the door was locked. Jeffrey was inside busily brushing his teeth and washing his face – at the same time.

Humphrey, still yawning, ambled to the kitchen to put the kettle on when he heard the toilet flush and the bathroom door open. He dashed back to the hall only to see a foamy-mouthed Jeffrey emerge from the bathroom and a streak of light tan – known as Godfrey – enter it and slam the door shut.

Humphrey sighed and returned to the kitchen. So far, this morning was just another typical start of the day for the Furricious Gang.

Little did Humphrey know that today was to be different.

The weather outside was dull and overcast. The sort of weather that teddy bears actually like. Feral, or wild, teddy bears like this weather because the subdued light makes it harder for people to spot them. Domesticated teddy bears like this weather because people tend to cuddle them more. They can be warm, cuddly and comforting.

Hot weather is not so great and wet weather is somewhat worse, so overcast is the best compromise and, like the rest of England, Godalming was often overcast. That is why a lot of teddy bears like to live in Britain and Ireland.

Of course, the Irish and Scottish bears have to be a bit more careful. In particular the West Coast Irish and Highland bears have to cope with high winds every now and then, and bears are quite light and not very aerodynamic.

There is the story of Ted O'Sullivan from County Kerry, in the hills just south of Dunquin. One day he and his girlfriend, a teddy bear called Ciara, decided to fly a kite because it was quite breezy, but not dangerously so, or so it seemed at the time.

They ran to the top of the hill and launched Ted's favourite kite and were amazed at how high they could get it. It flew higher and higher until Ted realised that the wind was picking up and a storm was coming in from the Atlantic. Unwilling to lose such a good kite Ted pulled and pulled, frantically rewinding the string in an attempt to bring it down. Ciara held on to him to prevent him from being blown away, but a gust of wind blew her hat askew, and she let go of him to adjust it.

Ted was snatched up into the air, still winding the string for all he was worth and did not realise that Ciara was calling up to him to return right this minute! Not that he could.

Ted drifted a considerable distance before finally landing in a donkey sanctuary in County Cork. He was unaware that he now held the record for the longest ever Irish kite flight. It took him days to walk back to his beloved Ciara only to find that she'd moved in with his neighbour because, as she explained, she thought he'd flown the coop and abandoned her.

Despite his pointing out that they lived in a small, camouflaged caravan (and quite a cosy one at that) and not a chicken-themed hut at all, she remained firm in her resolve. Besides, her new partner had no truck with kites.

All turned out well though, because Ciara's much larger sister, Sinéad, moved in with Ted and being a significantly heavier and a more insecure teddy bear (she would often ask him: 'Does my bum look even bigger if I wear this hat?') she never, ever, let go of him and to this day the pair hold the record for highest kite flights this side of Istanbul. At least for bears.

The Highland story is a little different. Mathan MacDonald acquired his first bear-sized tartan kilt (in fact it was an old discarded tartan pelmet) and wrapped it around him in true Scottish style. He proudly strutted around the Scottish Highlands showing it off to his friends. Then, one evening after a drinking session in the local pub, he declared he would unwrap himself and show his audience how he could turn his kilt into a warm sleeping blanket.

But he did this slowly, while at the same time dancing erotically and winking seductively at his friends' female partners. Then he made the mistake of asking if any of the ladies would like to join him in his warm sleeping blanket. This did not, in any way, endear him to his pals.

Subsequently, he was dragged outside just as the mountain wind picked up. Fortunately for Mathan it filled his half-unwrapped kilt like a sail and whisked him away from, what would have been, his 'physically persuasive' lesson in manners across the mountains.

His friends, in true Scottish tradition, rather than search for their colleague, preferred instead to raise a toast to that departed, lecherous bear. It runs as follows...

> May Mathan MacDonald, the kilted sky-bound bear
> Who mooned us all so breezily
> Be found no worse for underwear
> With his kilt and a new sense of decency
>
> But should he return with no finesse
> Still feeling ever so frisky
> We'll kick that bear stud to Inverness
> And to that, let's drink more whisky!

Mathan MacDonald landed a job on an oil rig in the North Sea. Literally.

Humphrey had finally had his turn in the bathroom and was getting ready for the morning's walk when the telephone on the hallway wall started trilling. He heard Godfrey pick up the handset.

"Hullo," said Godfrey.

A moment's silence, then... "This is Godfrey."

Another moment's silence, then... "I'll see if he's got out of bed yet," and returned the phone to its cradle with a click.

Humphrey arrived at the phone. "I'm *not* in bed. You've hung up. Why did you hang up?"

"Yes," said Godfrey.

"Who was it? Did you get their name?"

"She said she wanted to speak to you. She said she was Simport Ant."

"Never heard of her... oh wait a minute! She said it was important?"

"No. She said it was called Simport Ant. I didn't know ants could use a telephone."

The phone rang again, and Humphrey managed to grab it before he could strangle the youngster.

"Hello. This is Humphrey. How can I... yes... yes... no... no... I see... I don't see... oh dear... oh no... oh dear... oh no... uhm... do I have to?" Then he hung up and sat down on the floor.

"You've sitted on the floor," said Godfrey.

"No, I haven't. Not yet anyway. But I might do when all this sinks in. Oh dear," sighed Humphrey.

Jeffrey emerged from his bedroom ready to go for the walk.

"Why are you sitting on the floor?"

"I've just had a call from B.U.I.S.C.I.T.," said Humphrey.

"Uh oh," said Jeffrey.

"What's B.U.S..., B.I.C... What's that?" asked Godfrey.

"It's the British Ursine Intelligence Service, Civilian Intelligence Team. They are renowned for keeping teddy bears safe, sending teddy bears to their doom, and bad spelling." Humphrey put his head in his paws. "And they've just informed me that I've got to dispose of a vampire."

***

The alarm clock rang out and woke Vladimir Laraduc from his dream of flying high over the town of Godalming in the middle of the night. His dreams were nothing if not monochrome. He reached out of his coffin, tapped the clock's off button, switched off the electric blanket and sat up. He was already fully dressed in his black suit, white shirt and red-lined cape.

He cursed the fact that he couldn't check himself in the mirror. He knew he looked pretty cool even at the worst of times, but it would be nice to be sure. He wiped his nose with a handkerchief. Being a vampire was one thing but being a vampire with a bogie sticking out of a nostril somehow wouldn't have the same blood-curdling effect.

He walked to the bedroom window. Vladimir loved being a creature of death, and a particularly melodramatic one at that. Thinking he'd make a good actor he once applied for a position as a vampire in a Christmas pantomime, but didn't get the part because of, what the director called, his 'hamming it up'. The director only lived long enough to regret that decision.

Vladimir opened the curtains with a sudden swish and looked out at the potential victims milling about in his new hunting grounds. It was like a smorgasbord of arterial delights spread out before him. Even though it was night-time and dark outside he could see quite clearly, for vampires much preferred the night shift. So much so, they had adapted to it.

He recalled the time he stayed in one of those hotels that had vertical blinds instead of proper curtains. His dramatic swipe ended up with him entangled in the damned thing. That was embarrassing. He vowed never to stay in one of those hotels again.

What he didn't know was that the person in charge of standardising the hotel chain's decor, was a closet werewolf. But that's another story.

In the supermarket's car park a rather plump young man headed toward his BMW pushing a shopping trolley. 'Ah. Dinner,' thought Vladimir. He opened the window and dived out, trans-morphing into a bat as he did so.

On the roof above three pairs of eyes watched as the bat flew away.

"Right then. We're on," whispered Humphrey, wearing his Patent Black Ninja Special Forces Stealth Mission Abseiling Harness (Size: Adventurous Toddler). "We'll rappel down and enter the window. I'll go first. Is everyone ready?"

"Yes! I've improved my equipment and I'm going to be the fastest ninja bear in Godalming," said Jeffrey, keen as always.

"I'm cold," said Godfrey. "Has anyone got a snack?"

"Jeffrey, you deal with the curtains. I'll handle the clock. Godfrey, don't forget the jar."

And they jumped.

***

Now feeling satiated, and because it was such a pleasant evening, Vladimir decided to enjoy the night air and the deserted streets and walked back to his apartment. He let himself through the front door, poured himself a glass of red wine (apparently red goes best with blood) and wondered if Netflix had any decent new films, preferably not ones about vampires or werewolves. They were so inaccurate.

He entered his bedroom to close the window but stopped short. In the dark he could make out the recognisable silhouette of round ears on a round head sitting on his coffin.

"Hello," said Humphrey.

"Who are you?"

"Humphrey. A teddy bear. One of the Furricious Gang. A wool and fluff-based lifeform that has evolved immunity from vampires."

"What do you want?"

"I want you to move away. You are not welcome here."

"Is it because I is a vampire?"

"Definitely. Yes. It is."

"That is racism that is."

"Not if you're munching on people's necks, giving them scars, spreading diseases and sometimes eating them.

Unless you become a vegetarian with immediate effect, then I must insist you leave. For your own welfare, if not ours."

"I could kill you where you sit."

"But you know that would be pointless. Right?"

"I refuse to leave. You and your feeble fluffy fluff-based brain cannot make me. Besides, you needs me to feast upon the souls of the loud and aggressive youths that are taking the drugs, tearing up the streets late at night, vandalising the bus stops, and keeping the adults and the children awake with their loud motorcycles and their loud, loathsome music."

"This is Godalming. We don't get much of that around here." Humphrey thought for a moment. "Don't you get affected by the drugs at all? You know, when you suck it up?"

Vladimir bobbed his head from side to side. "Erm, sometimes..." He smiled. "Sometimes... you know, it adds a little spice once in a while. It makes life a little more... interesting. Especially the psychedelic ones. I love the psychedelic ones. I remember once..."

"You must decide to leave now, or we shall be forced to take serious action. You have enough money, right?"

"Ha, ha, ha, ha. A fluffy teddy bear threatening to take serious action against a powerful vampire! Of course I has enough money you insignificant little piece of fluff! The pension laws in this country were especially designed by Goths like us. I has money. Much money. So be gone with you. You ineffectual pest! I has spoken and now you must be living with the knowledge that I shall be ruling the night in

this town. Now be gone. I wants to watch a movie before the sun is rising."

Humphrey stood up, climbed the rope to the windowsill and attached his descender gear to it. He turned to face the vampire.

"I am Humphrey of the Furricious Gang. I have asked you politely to leave us in peace and warned you of consequences. Will you not reconsider?"

"Be gone you irrelevant, fluffy speck of bloodless filth. You are no threat to me. Be gone!"

And so Humphrey dropped out of sight.

***

The alarm clock rang out and woke Vladimir Laraduc from his dream of flying over the town of Godalming. He reached out of his coffin, tapped the clock's off button, switched off the electric blanket and sat up. He was still dressed in his black suit, white shirt and red-lined cape.

He wiped his nose with a handkerchief and walked to the bedroom window. Vladimir threw open the curtains with a dramatic swish and...

He screamed.

The afternoon sun shone brightly through the window, cooking the vampire's flesh. He frantically tried to pull the curtains closed again but they were stuck and would not budge.

In his struggles he knocked an unseen glass jar of some liquid off the windowsill. It smashed coating the oak floor with a strong garlic solution causing the vampire to choke and clasp at his melting throat. He staggered, slipped and fell into the pool of poison.

Before he completely melted away, the last thing Vladimir saw was a post-it note stuck to the side of the fallen jar. It read...

'Beware the fluffy!'

Humphrey, Jeffrey and Godfrey

The Amazon Parcel

"Humpy. There's a woodpecker trying to make a nest in our front door." The little teddy bear, known as Godfrey, was in the shower room tilting his head in puzzlement and frowning at the older bear. Humphrey was in the shower standing on one leg and only wearing his shower cap, two little showerproof ear caps on his ears, and nothing else while blissfully loofaring his back and at the same time failing to sing Wuthering Heights in anything like the right key. Or the right tune. Or even with the right words.

Humphrey's head spun around to look at the intruder. His foot caught the soap and with friction-free effort he pirouetted a full circle before falling over shooting the soap out and missing Godfrey's head by a finger-width.

"Ow!" He dropped the loofah and covered his private parts with his paws. "Don't you ever to think of knocking before coming in here?" he snapped. He attempted to make a grab for the shower curtain but couldn't reach.

Godfrey thought for a moment then shook his head.

"Go back to the front door and tell them to go away."

The little one left. Humphrey crawled out of the shower and dried himself. After a short time there was a knock on the shower room door, but again Godfrey didn't wait and came straight in.

"Godfrey! You should wait outside until I *say* you can come in," said Humphrey, hastily covering his nether regions again.

"Why?"

"Because it's not polite to barge in. I might have been... doing something."

Godfrey crinkled his nose. Catching Humphrey wailing something unintelligible into the shower head would surely count as 'doing something'. But he chose to stay quiet anyway.

Humphrey sighed. "Have they gone?"

"He says he's not a woodpecker but a parcel from the amazing something."

Humphrey frowned. This sounded like a mistake. He hadn't ordered anything to be delivered... unless Jeffrey had ordered something and not let him know. He ordered the little one out of the shower room, quickly got dressed, and brushed his ears. The two of them went back to the front door. Humphrey left a trail of damp footsteps behind him - because teddy bears don't dry that quickly. It's something to do with their fluff being very absorbent, which is also why very few teddy bears are ever seen in a rugby team's shower room.

***

She was known to her peers as Princess Sabriella the Black, Tormentor of Souls, Slasher of Demons, Terror of the Night, and Prowler of Nightmares. To the old witch that owned her she was known as Puddles. Despite being a mere three hundred years old, which was young for a familiar,

when it came to house training the cat still had a lot to
learn.

They both lived in their pretty little country cottage on the outskirts of Godalming. It had started life as a set of fifteenth century alms houses built by the local lord of the manor. They were built in order to prove to his would-be wife that he was a thoughtful and considerate man. He wasn't, but two months after the lord's wedding he died leaving her a much happier, and somewhat wiser, widow.

The alms buildings had then been remodelled in the sixteenth century by a wandering knight. He wasn't very good at explaining himself (words were very difficult for him) but he had discovered that a swinging sword would express his desires very clearly. For instance, it came in particularly useful when convincing the poor and elderly to abandon their homes. It was also a great help to get the local builder to renovate them and convert them into a single dwelling at an amazing discount. And finally, it acted as an efficient sympathy-enhancing device for the local judiciary and enabled them to see his side of the story without him needing to use any words at all.

The knight, whose name has since been lost to time, had found that his purchase of such an impressive sword had given him an amazingly good return on investment.

The buildings were next acquired by an up-and-coming sheep trader. As his wealth grew, he extensively remodelled the cottage, so much so that its early fifteenth-century origin was completely lost and these days it is considered to be a seventeenth-century dwelling. This is just as well because the earlier house had not been built very well and bits tended to fall off it. Particularly those bits where a swinging sword had been used to express the owner's feelings.

The cottage was then acquired by, apparently, a young man for him and his new wife. After several weeks the young man disappeared, but the young lady, who must have been very distraught at his departure, acquired a sad-looking pet frog to comfort her. She was often seen talking to it, and sometimes scolding it too. The young man was never seen again.

Some weeks later she acquired the black cat known to her peers as Princess Sabriella the Black, Tormentor of Souls, Slasher of Demons, Terror of the Night, and Prowler of Nightmares. Shortly thereafter the frog disappeared too.

The witch, who still lives near to Godalming (so we shan't call her by her pretend name - instead we'll call her by her witch's name which is Ms Belladonna Cadaveretta Fridgamortis) is a minor celebrity in her profession. It was she who invented the elixir that led to an ancient man discovering that snails could be edible, a Chinese peasant to discover that certain birds' nests worked well in soups, a French monk to discover that frogs' legs are edible, and later a German scientist (Justus von Liebig) to discover that a strong sticky by-product of beer brewing could also be edible, especially if spread on bread or used in cooking. But, as for the latter item, even to this day, people's opinions are strongly divided.

Her elixir is often used by witches around the world to cast spells that trick humans into doing things which they wouldn't have done otherwise. It formed one of the base components for love potions, potions that made knights believe they could slay dragons single-handedly, and lemmings to believe they had wings and could fly.

Ms Fridgamortis had since discovered the possibility of a new elixir and was keen to rekindle her fame. For this she needed a special and rare herb from the Amazon rainforest but was horrified to learn that the rainforest was being burned for industry profit. She vowed she would do something about these pesky, selfish people.

***

Humphrey, Jeffrey and Godfrey were in the living room looking intently at the cardboard box. Then Humphrey had an idea.

"Jeffrey. Give me a hand pulling this parcel into the garage. We'll open it and see what it is before we deliver it." He turned to the smallest bear. "Godfrey. I have a special mission for you. Can you deliver a message to Princess Layer of the scribbles? Say the following: 'We have to deliver an Amazon parcel to the sorceress. I will pay you.' Can you remember that?"

Godfrey nodded.

"Good. Don't forget it now. Off you go." And Godfrey departed on his new mission.

It took a while for Godfrey to find a scribble. The little animal was inside a litter bin rummaging through the rubbish looking for something to eat or trade.

"Ahem!" said Godfrey. The scribble's head popped out of the bin and looked at the little bear.

"What do you want? I'm busy."

"Can you tell the Princess Slayer that we must deliver an amazing package to a sorcerer. Humphrey will pay you."

The scribble's ears perked up. "He'll pay me? How much?" Without waiting for an answer, she called out,

"Follow me!" and leaped out of the bin and along the field until they came to a bush. "Come on!" She waved for Godfrey to follow.

Under the bush, hidden from view, were two guard scribbles, guarding an entrance to an old, abandoned rabbit burrow.

"Halt! Who goes... oh it's you, Patme Armordillo. What do you want?"

"This bear came to me and said that we should give an amazing thing to a sorcerer. Humphrey is going to pay for it."

The guard looked at Godfrey, then at the scribble. "Follow me. I'll introduce you to the princess."

All three entered the burrow and travelled down dank tunnels deep into the ground. Godfrey had to stoop all the way because, despite being a short bear, he was taller than the scribbles.

They arrived at a door. The guard opened it and entered the room.

"Don't you ever think of knocking before coming in here?" screamed Princess Layer, making a grab for an item of clothing. "I might have been... doing something."

The guard thought for a moment then shook his head.

"Go outside and wait!"

The guard left the room and closed the door.

"What do you want?" called the princess from within the royal chamber.

"We have a message from Humphrey of the Furricious
Gang. He says we could put something amazing in a sauce

and he will play with you if you want."

There was a moment's silence before the door opened a crack and the queen peered around it.

"He wants to play with me?"

"Apparently," said the guard.

"And he's going to pay me," said the scribble known as Patme Armordillo.

The princess looked at Godfrey and raised her tiny eyebrows.

Godfrey gulped. "Uhm. Err... Humpy said he got an amazing parcel and he uhm, told me to tell you that it was amazingly saucy, and so he wanted you to pay for it."

The scribble princess grew angry and stamped her foot. "Those pesky delivery drivers! They've delivered it to the wrong address again." She disappeared inside her chamber and called out to the guard. "Get ten more guards and prepare an expedition to the bowling green. Bring weapons. We'll sort this cheeky bear out!"

***

The expedition of scribbles and Godfrey arrived at the Furricious Gang's front door. The princess nodded to one of her guards. He smiled and winked back at her.

"No, you fool! Knock on the bear's door."

"Oh, sorry."

The scribble sidled up to the door and knocked on it. There was a moment's pause before a voice called out, "Who is it?"

"It's me. Hang Solow."

"We're busy right now. Can you come back later?"

The Princess barged her way forward. "Stand back! This is Princess Layer. I demand you open the door!"

"I can't open it if I stand back. I can't reach it. We're only teddy bears and our arms aren't that long."

"Not you! You fool. I want you to open the door. Now!"

"Okay."

The door opened a little and Jeffrey poked his nose around it.

"Hello, Godfrey. Did you deliver the message?"

"Yes," said Godfrey, but with an uneasy feeling that something was amiss somewhere.

"What is your name?" demanded the Princess.

"No, it isn't. My name is Jeffrey, not Watt."

"Don't be cheeky with me, you young ragamuffin! I am Princess Layer of the Scribbles."

"I'm not a rag of muffling, I'm a teddy bear." Jeffrey's literal mind was not helping to calm down the princess.

She barely stopped herself from screaming at the young bear.

"Fetch Humphrey for me. Now!" She demanded.

"Okay." And the door closed.

At that point Snowy and Woof, who were carrying a bag of beetfruit, arrived. Seeing the armed scribbles and hearing how angry the princess was they decided to stay back, sit down, and watch from a safe distance. And while they were at it, they shared some of the beetfruit. They were sure that Humphrey would have approved of such a spontaneous picnic.

Some moments later the door opened, and Humphrey came out with some sticky tape dangling from his ear.

"Hello, Princess. Good to see..." He didn't get to finish the greeting. With a very unprincess-like kick between the legs, she floored the poor bear.

"Oof," squeaked Humphrey. Snowy and Woof winced too, thankful they weren't involved.

"Godfrey informs me that you have received one of my parcels. In it is something very saucy which you want me to wear so you can play with me. And you want me to pay for it all. That's blackmail! And you tried to bribe one of my scribbles too."

Not surprisingly, Humphrey looked confused.

"Well?" demanded the princess. "What do you have to say for yourself?"

Humphrey staggered upright but he did catch Godfrey sneaking in the door.

"I think there's been a misunderstanding," he managed, still gasping for air from the shock of the kick.

To cut a long story short, Humphrey had to explain to the irate princess that the message she received was not what he had originally said. He apologised profusely, many times, and even took her inside to show her the parcel and its contents. Patme Armordillo was deeply disappointed that she wouldn't be paid, and Princess Layer was happy that she wasn't being blackmailed and didn't have to pay anything - but was secretly disappointed that Humphrey had no intention to play with her after all.

Still, she had managed to kick Humphrey where it hurts and get away with it. That was a tick in her bucket list and put her in a better mood.

Snowy and Woof didn't get to hear the explanation, only the accusations. For weeks after that several scandalous rumours circulated around Godalming, each juicier than the last. The Furricious Gang, and Humphrey in particular, acquired an ill-deserved reputation.

Godfrey had gone to hide in his bedroom, which was just as well because everyone blamed him for the mix-up.

"Why won't you take it to the witch yourself?" asked the princess when all had calmed down.

"Because she's a cuddle monkey," explained Humphrey. "Whenever she sees one of us teddy bears, she grabs us and hugs us to her chest and doesn't let go for hours."

"What's so bad about that?"

"Her cat gets jealous."

"Oooh," sighed the princess. "That explains a lot. You do *not* want to get onto the wrong side of Princess Sabriella. She can be one nasty cat."

"And she has sharp claws."

"So why did the witch have the parcel delivered here?"

"Jeffrey and I think it's a rare herb from the Amazonian rainforest. She doesn't want it to be traced back to her."

"I see." Thinking of blackmail and the value of the parcel to the sorceress, but not thinking of the possible consequences, Princess Layer thought of a plan.

"We'll deliver it for you. For a fee," she declared.

"Great! Ten digestives?"

"No. Ten chocolate ones."

"Ooh. How about we meet halfway. Let's say five chocolate ones."

"No. Ten full-sized digestive biscuits."

"Ooh, that's expensive. I don't know... How about ten plain digestive biscuits?"

"Agreed!" and they shook paws on the deal.

The scribbles got the contract to deliver the Amazon parcel to one Ms Belladonna Cadaveretta Fridgamortis of Godalming. Sadly, Princess Layer tried to pull a fast one and sell it to the wise old witch to make a better profit on the deal. This made the witch very angry, which also made her cat, Princess Sabriella the Black, Tormentor of Souls, Slasher of Demons, Terror of the Night, and Prowler of Nightmares (also known as Puddles) pretty angry too.

The witch cast a spell.

***

The scribbles no longer live on the Lammas Lands or the Phillips Memorial Park. No one knows where they are now. If you search for a scribble in Godalming, you'll be hard pressed to find one. You may find some squirrels, but none of them look skinny, greasy and unkempt like a proper scribble. Humphrey hopes they managed to escape to somewhere safe like the woods near Compton, or maybe to the woods south of Peperharow Road. If you go walking in those woods let me know if you see one.

But most importantly remember, if you ever need a message delivering, it's best to write it down. Sometimes the message might be misunderstood, or even changed. Especially if you rely on a little bear to do it for you.